First Revised Edition

Printed in the United States of America

ISBN 1-57082-141-0

10 9 8 7 6 5 4 3 2 1

Adapted by
Joey Green

Illustrated by
Vaccaro Associates, Inc.

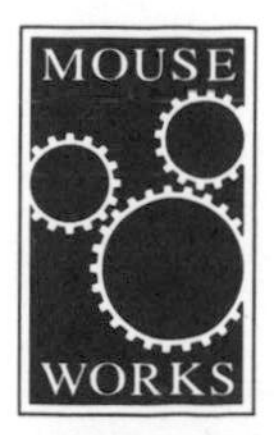

# Contents

## The Man in the Sand

All the Babies love to play in the sandbox on a sunny day. Baby Mickey dug with a purple spoon. Baby Minnie built castles with a blue cup. Baby Daisy dug with her hands. Baby Goofy filled a red pail with sand. Baby Pluto just dug and dug with his paws.

Baby Mickey found a big blue block in the sand. "Mine!" he yelled.
Baby Minnie found a red bow in the sand. "Mine!" she yelled.

Baby Daisy found a white ball with a happy face. “Mine!” she yelled.
Baby Goofy found a purple hat with a green stripe. “Mine!” he yelled.
Baby Pluto just scratched and scratched. He was all full of sand.
But soon all the Babies got tired of playing alone. They decided to play together.

Baby Mickey put his block down in the sand.
Baby Daisy put the white ball with the happy face on top.
Baby Minnie put her bow on the blue block.
Baby Goofy put his purple hat on top.
"Look!" said Baby Mickey, "a little man!"
But best of all, Baby Pluto found his bone in the sand. He thought his bone was the best toy of all!

# Hide and Seek

Close your eyes!
    Do not peek!
We are playing
    Hide and seek.

Baby Donald
    Counts to ten.
Baby Mickey
    Hides again.

"Hooray! I found you!"
    Donald cheers.
"You forgot
    To hide your ears!"

# The Baby Who Didn't Like Spinach

Baby Horace did not like to eat spinach.
"Spinach is yucky!" he said.
So he threw it out the window. Uh-oh!
The spinach landed all over
his friend Baby Troll.

"Why did you do that?" asked Baby Troll.

"I do not like spinach," said Baby Horace.

"Come to my house," said Baby Troll.
"And you will never have to eat
spinach again."

Baby Horace went to Baby Troll's house. They played all day. When it was time for dinner, Baby Troll put two bowls of twigs and leaves on the table.

"Yummy, yummy," said Baby Troll. "I love to eat twigs and leaves."

"Ewww! Yuck!" said Baby Horace. "I'm not going to eat twigs and leaves!" And he threw the twigs and leaves out the window.

Baby Troll could not believe it. How could anyone not like twigs and leaves?

"I know," said Baby Troll. "How about some mud pie?"

"Ewww! Yuck!" said Baby Horace. "This mud pie tastes just like mud!"

"It is!" said Baby Troll. "Isn't it yummy?"

"Not to me," said Baby Horace. And he threw the mud pie out the window and ran back home.

When Baby Horace got home, he asked his mother for dinner.

"All we have is spinach," his mother said.

Baby Horace was so happy. "Spinach tastes better than twigs and leaves," he said. "And it's much better than mud pie!"

Baby Horace ate all the spinach in his bowl. And he never threw anything out the window again!

## The Make-Believe Parade

Baby Donald was dreaming about a parade. He could see the clowns. He could hear the horns and drums. He could taste the popcorn. He wanted a balloon!

All of a sudden, Baby Donald heard some noise in the hall. *Bang! Bam! Boom!* He crawled over to see what was happening.

Baby Daisy was waving a flag. It was red, white, and blue. Baby Minnie was twirling a long wooden spoon.

So Baby Donald followed them.

All the Babies were making lots of noise in the kitchen.
Baby Mickey blew a horn. *Toot-toot!*
Baby Clarabelle blew a horn, too. *Toot-toot-toot!*
Baby Horace banged a pot with two spoons. *Boom! Boom!*
Baby Goofy made funny faces like a clown.
Baby Donald thought and thought. "What can I do?" he wondered.

Baby Donald knew just what to do. He found the lids of two pots and banged them together as loud as he could! *Clang!*
*Clang!*
*Clang!*

"Wow!" cheered the other Babies. "That sounds great!"

Then all the babies started following Baby Donald.

"Yay! Hooray!" said Baby Donald. "We're having a parade!"

# Too Much in My Tummy

First I ate an apple,
Then some chocolate cake.
I ate a lot of pudding,
a banana and a grape.

I really had too much to eat,
but everything was yummy.
Now the only problem is—
It really hurts my tummy.

# Splish! Splash!

Baby Mickey was sad and lonely. He was sitting on the swing in the park. But there was nobody else to play with. Suddenly he felt drops of water on his head. He looked up in the sky, but the sun was shining. "Where is the water coming from?" wondered Baby Mickey.

Baby Mickey turned around. A sprinkler was watering the grass. The sprinkler had made a puddle of water. “Oh, boy!” thought Baby Mickey. He sat in the puddle and wiggled his fingers in the mud. The mud felt squishy and funny.

When Baby Mickey crawled out of the puddle, he was very muddy and sticky. The freshly cut grass stuck to Baby Mickey. He looked very silly. Then he saw Baby Goofy. "Hi, Baby Goofy, would you like to play?"

Baby Goofy was very scared. His eyes opened wide. "Oh my gawrsh!" yelled Baby Goofy. "A green monster!"

"It's only me," said Baby Mickey. "Don't be scared!"

Baby Goofy and Baby Mickey played together in the mud. Baby Goofy wasn't scared anymore. Baby Mickey wasn't sad and lonely. When they went home, they were both so muddy, they took a bubble bath together. It was a very nice day.

# Hello, Dolly

Baby Daisy has a dolly.
Baby Minnie has one, too.
It is really so amazing
What those little dolls can do.

Daisy's dolly does a dance.
Minnie's dolly goes to bed.
Baby Daisy combs the hair
On her little dolly's head.

Then the dollies play alone.
But when they are done,
Both the dollies play together.
That's always much more fun.

# The Choo-Choo Train

Baby Goofy and Baby Clarabelle were going for a ride on a choo-choo train. The train was red and blue.
The conductor wore a bright blue jacket and hat. “Tickets, please,” he said.
Baby Clarabelle gave the conductor her ticket.
Baby Goofy was scared. He closed his eyes and held out his ticket.

“Don’t be afraid,” said the conductor. “The choo-choo train is fun! All aboard!”

The conductor was right. The choo-choo train was fun.

The engineer drove the train. *Chugga-chugga-chugga!*

He rang the bell. *Ding-a-ding-a-ding!*

He blew the whistle. *Choo! Choo!*

The train went on a bridge over a river. Baby Goofy and Baby Clarabelle saw donkeys and horses.

Smoke blew from the train.

The train went through a tunnel, over another bridge, and into a western town.

Two cowboys were dancing outside a general store. "Yahoo!" they shouted.

The train went round and round. Then it began to slow down.

The train stopped at the station. The train ride was over.

Baby Goofy did not want to get out of the train. He was having too much fun.

"Tickets, please," said the conductor.

Oh no! Baby Goofy and Baby Clarabelle did not have any more tickets. That meant no more train rides!

Suddenly Baby Mickey got on the train.

"Look!" he said. "I have three tickets: one for me, one for Baby Clarabelle, and one for Baby Goofy!"

"Thank you, Baby Mickey," said Baby Clarabelle and Baby Goofy.

The engineer let Baby Goofy sit on his lap and blow the whistle. *Choo! Choo!*

"I love the choo-choo train," said Baby Goofy. And the three friends went off on another train ride together.

# All the Fixin's

Baby Horace loved to work at his workbench. He loved to fix all the toys. He was working very hard. He was trying to fix his truck.

Baby Clarabelle wanted to play with Baby Horace. She threw her big blue ball at him. She wanted to get his attention.

Baby Horace did not like to get hit with a ball. He didn't have any time for games. There were too many toys to fix.

Baby Horace heard Baby Minnie crying. Her teddy bear had ripped open. Teddy's stuffing was popping out of his tummy.

Baby Horace knew something had to be done. Teddy had to be fixed right away, before all the stuffing came out of his tummy.

Baby Horace brought Teddy to his workbench. He had never fixed a teddy bear before. He didn't know what to do.

First he tried his hammer. Then he tried his screwdriver, his pliers, and his wrench. But nothing worked.

Baby Clarabelle just laughed and laughed. "Silly Baby Horace! That's no way to fix a teddy bear," said Baby Clarabelle.

Baby Clarabelle got her sewing basket and sewed up the teddy bear. Baby Horace couldn't believe his eyes. Baby Clarabelle could fix toys too!
"Why don't we fix toys together?" asked Baby Horace.
"I'd love to help you!" said Baby Clarabelle. "And I'll never hit you with my ball again!"
So from that day on, Baby Clarabelle and Baby Horace fixed toys together.
When they were done, they played ball with the big blue ball.

## Funny Faces

When Baby Horace wears a mask
He pretends that he's a fish,
A bird, a pig, a dog, or cat,
Or an elephant, if you wish.

## Raindrops

Raindrops tap my windows,
The wind bumps on my doors.
It's raining down on my house.
Is it raining down on yours?

It's warm by the fireplace,
All nice and safe indoors.
It's cozy warm in my house.
Is it cozy warm in yours?

## The Treasure

Baby Donald and Baby Daisy were digging with shovels on a beach called Pirate's Cove. Baby Donald found a shoe in the sand. Baby Daisy found some shells. Then they both found a treasure chest.

"Ahoy, mateys," said a parrot sitting on the shoulder of a pirate. The pirate wore a black hat with a red feather, a black jacket and red pants.

"That's my treasure," said the pirate. "I buried that treasure chest here a long time ago."

"Oops," said Baby Donald and Baby Daisy.

The pirate opened the treasure chest. Baby Donald and Baby Daisy wanted to see gold coins and jewels. But the treasure chest wasn't filled with coins or jewels. Inside were beach toys and a big beach ball.

The pirate told them he had buried the treasure chest on the beach when he was a little boy. The pirate played catch with Baby Donald and Baby Daisy. Then they all played in the sand with the shovel and pail. They had a lot of fun together.

"It's time to bury the treasure chest again," said the parrot.

"We have to hide it for the next time we come back to play," said the pirate.

After they buried the treasure chest, the pirate said farewell. "Just remember, friends are the best treasures on earth," he said. "Bye-bye!"

"Bye-bye," said Baby Donald and Baby Daisy.

"Bye-bye," said the parrot.

Baby Donald and Baby Daisy couldn't wait to come back to Pirate's Cove and play again.

## Sleepyhead

Baby Gus sleeps day and night.
But do you think that is right?
Wake up, you silly sleepyhead.
Who wants to spend their
life in bed?

## Rainbow

At the end of every rainbow
    There's a pot of shining gold.
And I want to find it
    Before I'm three years old.

But when I look up in the sky
    And see a rainbow bend,
I always have to wonder why
    They never say which end.

# Mr. Sandman

Baby Mickey was very tired, but he did not want to go to sleep. His eyes felt heavy, but he would not let them close.

"Sleepy time," said a voice. Baby Mickey looked up to find a little man sitting on his bed.

"I am the Sandman," said the little man. "Close your eyes and hold my hand," he said, "and I will take you to Sand Land."

Baby Mickey closed his eyes, and suddenly he and Mr. Sandman were in a strange land where everything was made from sand. Giant sand castles were everywhere. "Wow!" said Baby Mickey.

Baby Mickey played in the sand. He wanted to make more sand castles. All of a sudden a little man made from sand popped up from the sand.

"My name is Sandy," said the little man made from sand. "Would you like to play with me?"

Baby Mickey and Sandy played together, making sand castles and digging tunnels.

Suddenly the wind began to blow the sand into a great big sandstorm. Baby Mickey closed his eyes.

When Baby Mickey opened his eyes again, he was back in his own bed. "That was fun," he thought. "But where are my new friends?" Then he sighed. Maybe it was all a dream. Maybe there was no Sandman at all.

Baby Mickey sat up in bed and rubbed his eyes. There was sand in his hands.

So it wasn't a dream after all. Baby Mickey could visit the Sandman whenever he went to sleep. That made Mickey very, very happy.

# Up and Down

Here we are,
Halfway there,
Sitting on
The middle stair.

Pardon me
For not knowing.
I forgot
Where we're going.

Can you tell me,
little pup—
Are we climbing
Down . . . or up?

# Rock Around the Blocks

Baby Donald loved to play with blocks. Baby Clarabelle, Baby Goofy, and Baby Horace watched Baby Donald make a tall building with all the different colored blocks. Baby Donald used yellow blocks, red blocks, green blocks, and purple blocks. He used pink blocks, white blocks, and orange blocks.

"Whee!" said Baby Goofy. He touched the tall building and it fell over. It was an accident.

"Boo-hoo!" cried Baby Donald.

Baby Goofy was very sorry. He tried to make the tall building again.

"No, no, no!" cried Baby Donald. "That's not the right way!" He did not want anyone to play with his blocks. He cried and cried.

Baby Clarabelle and Baby Horace helped Baby Goofy. Baby Clarabelle built a corral for her toy horse. Baby Goofy built a pyramid with one yellow block on the top. Baby Horace built a road for his toy car.

"Wowee!" said Baby Donald. He was in a good mood again.

Then Baby Clarabelle, Baby Horace, and Baby Goofy knocked down all the blocks again. They laughed and laughed.

Now Baby Donald could help them build something new together.

They all started to build a big castle with a flag on top. It was much more fun to play together.

A baby's toys
Make lots of noise.
They honk, they quack, they ring.

Some, on wheels,
Make squeaks and squeals
When baby pulls the string.

Some sound chimes,
Or nursery rhymes.
Some tweet just like a bird.

That's why I love
My baseball glove.
It never says a word!

# Where's the White Ball?

Baby Mickey and Baby Minnie were visiting Old McDonald's farm.
They fed the ducks, they rode the ponies, and they played in the barn.

Now they were playing catch with a little white ball. Baby Mickey threw the white ball and it bounced away. Where did it go?

First Baby Mickey and Baby Minnie looked in the pigpen.

"Oink, oink," said the pigs, rolling in the mud.

They had not seen the little white ball.

Baby Mickey and Baby Minnie looked in the vegetable garden. They found orange carrots, red tomatoes, and green lettuce. But they did not find the little white ball.

Baby Mickey and Baby Minnie looked in the barn. They found a brown cow eating hay. "Moo!" said the cow. She had not seen the little white ball.

Baby Mickey saw a rooster sitting on the fence.

"Cock-a-doodle-doo!" crowed the rooster. But he had not seen the little white ball.

Baby Mickey saw a goat eating a boot. "Baahhhh!" said the goat. But he had not seen the little white ball.

Baby Minnie saw a pony. "Neigh!" said the pony. Old McDonald let Minnie feed the pony some sugar. But the pony had not seen the little white ball.

Baby Mickey and Baby Minnie went inside the henhouse.
All the hens were sitting on their nests.
"Cluck, cluck!" said one of the hens. Her name was Henrietta.
But Baby Mickey and Baby Minnie did not find the little white ball.

“Wait,” said Old McDonald. “I think Henrietta is trying to tell us something.”
“Cluck, cluck, cluck!” said Henrietta.
Old McDonald reached into Henrietta’s nest and pulled out something round and white.
Baby Mickey and Baby Minnie thought it was an egg. But it was not an egg. It was the little white ball.
“Hooray!” they yelled. Now they could play ball again.

# The Cookie Dragon

Once upon a time there was a big green dragon named Jeremy. He was very sad and lonely, because all the people in the town were afraid to visit him. So Jeremy made all kinds of things to keep himself busy. One day he decided to bake chocolate chip cookies.

Baby Gus was taking a nap under a tree in the forest when all of a sudden he smelled something delicious. He woke up right away. He had never smelled anything this wonderful before. Baby Gus followed the delicious smell through the forest to a cave. He wondered what the smell could be.

Inside the cave, Baby Gus found a tray of chocolate chip cookies sitting on a rock. He started to eat one. He did not know the cookies belonged to Jeremy the Dragon. Jeremy was very surprised. He never had a guest before.

"Who are you?" asked Jeremy the Dragon.

“I am Baby Gus,” said Baby Gus. “Will you be my friend?”

“But I am a dragon and you are a duck,” said Jeremy the Dragon.

“That’s okay,” said Baby Gus. “As long as we both love cookies and milk we’ll be best friends forever.”

So Baby Gus and Jeremy the Dragon became friends over cookies and milk, and Jeremy was never lonely again.

## Leave It to Fall

The leaves turn red and yellow
When fall comes around.
The wind then blows the leaves
off and they fall to the ground.

I pick up some of the leaves
And make a little stack.
The wind then blows them all
away just when I turn my back.

## Ode to a Piano

The piano is one of life's joys.
It's one of my favorite toys.
Though my fingers can't yet
Play a Bach minuet,
My fists make a wonderful noise.

# The Talking Ladybug

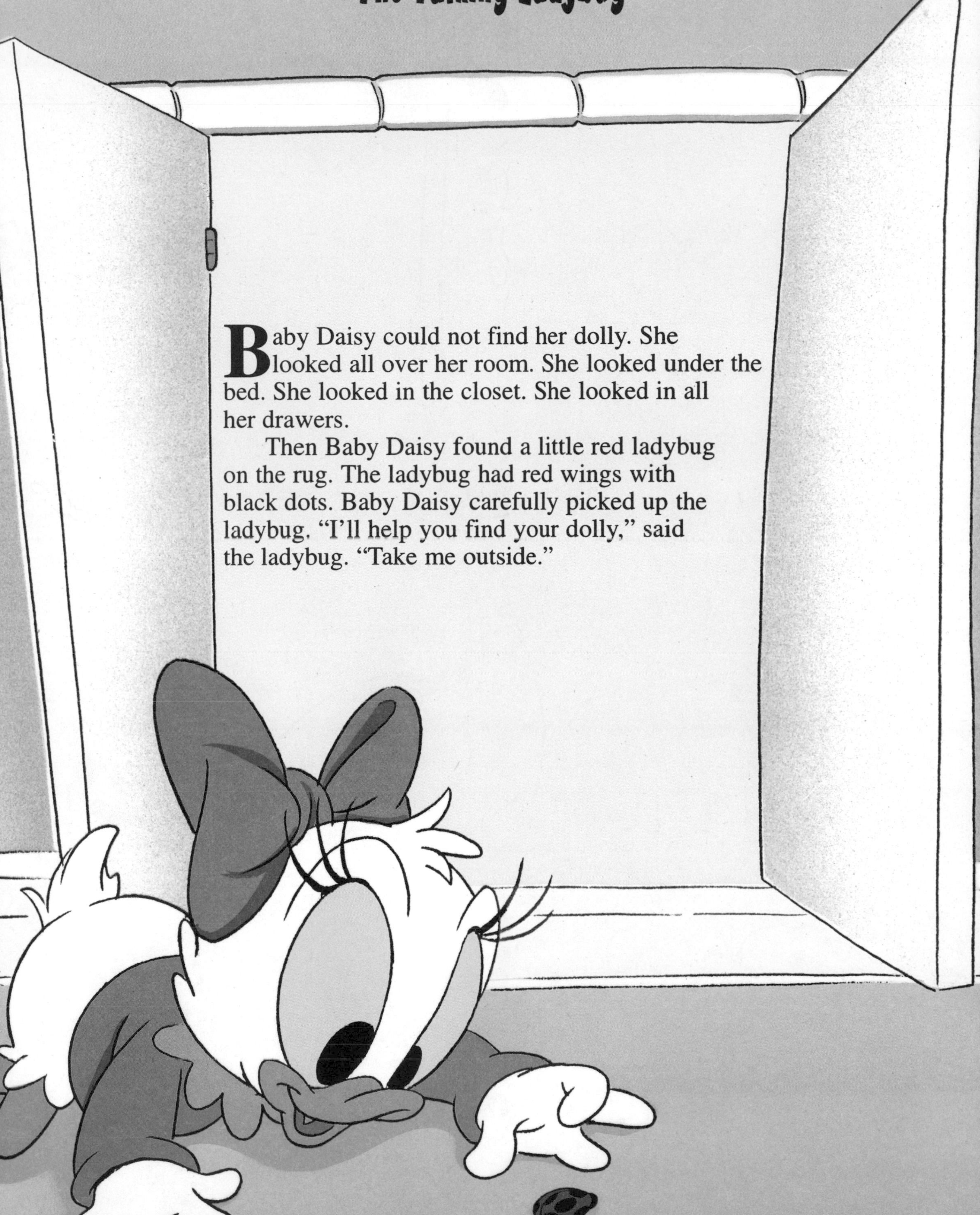

Baby Daisy could not find her dolly. She looked all over her room. She looked under the bed. She looked in the closet. She looked in all her drawers.

Then Baby Daisy found a little red ladybug on the rug. The ladybug had red wings with black dots. Baby Daisy carefully picked up the ladybug. "I'll help you find your dolly," said the ladybug. "Take me outside."

Baby Daisy had never heard a ladybug talk before. She wanted to find her dolly, so she took the ladybug outside.

Baby Daisy took the ladybug to the pretty pink plastic flamingo that stood on one leg. "Have you seen Baby Daisy's dolly?" the ladybug asked the flamingo.

"No," said the pink flamingo. "Ask the rosebush."

"Have you seen Baby Daisy's dolly?" the ladybug asked the rosebush.
"No," said the rosebush. "Ask the big oak tree."
Baby Daisy crawled over to the big oak tree. "Have you seen Baby Daisy's dolly?" the ladybug asked the tree.
"Yes," said the tree. "It's over by the white fence."

"Dolly!" shouted Baby Daisy.

The ladybug flew away. Baby Daisy was so happy to have her dolly again. "Bye-bye, ladybug," said Baby Daisy.

"Bye-bye, Baby Daisy," said the ladybug.

# If I Had a Dinosaur

If I had a dinosaur,
I think I'd name him Gus,
Then we'd go out for a ride.
We'd probably take a bus.

If I had a dinosaur,
We'd go swimming in the ocean.
If the sun got very hot,
We'd use lots of suntan lotion.

If I had a dinosaur
Bedtime would not be boring.
I don't think I'd get much sleep
If Gus did lots of snoring.

# The Castle

It was a beautiful summer day at the beach. Baby Mickey was throwing a frisbee for Baby Pluto. Baby Pete and Baby Goofy were playing catch with a big beach ball.

Baby Donald was sitting on a pink blanket. He didn't know what to do. Then Baby Donald got an idea! He would build a sand castle!

Baby Donald took his pail and found a spot on the beach. He dug in the sand and made his sand castle. He built two towers and a big wall around the castle.

Baby Donald was very proud of his sand castle. He crawled off to get the other Babies to show them his castle.

While Baby Donald was gone, a big wave came up from the ocean and washed his castle away.

When the Babies came to see Baby Donald's castle, it was all gone.

"Who took my sand castle?" wondered Baby Donald. He didn't know where his sand castle could be.

Maybe Baby Goofy had taken his sand castle.

He grabbed a pail from Baby Goofy and turned it upside down to look for his sand castle. Pretty shells fell out of the pail. "Mine," said Baby Goofy. He started to cry.

Baby Donald was sorry. He knew he shouldn't grab things away from someone else.

Just then a wave came up from the ocean and washed away all the shells. Now Baby Donald knew what had happened to his sand castle. The ocean had washed it away.

Baby Donald knew just what to do. He would build a new sand castle. This time he would build it away from the ocean. This time he would ask the other Babies to help him.

Baby Mickey brought pieces of driftwood. Baby Pete added seaweed. Baby Goofy collected lots of shells to decorate the new sand castle. Even Baby Pluto dug in the sand.

This was the best sand castle ever!

# The Little Red Sailboat

It was a beautiful, breezy day at the pond. Baby Mickey had a red sailboat. Baby Donald had a blue sailboat. Baby Minnie had a yellow sailboat. Baby Daisy had a green sailboat. All four sailboats had beautiful white sails.

The four Babies put their sailboats into the water and gave each a little push. The breeze blew the sails and away the boats went.

"Hooray!" everyone shouted.

The boats were having a race. The four friends crawled to the other side of the pond. They waited to see which sailboat would get to the other side first.

Minnie's yellow sailboat got there first. Then came Donald's blue sailboat. Then came Daisy's green sailboat.

But where was Mickey's red sailboat?

Baby Mickey couldn't play with his friends if he didn't have a sailboat. He was very sad.

Then he saw something red on the other side of the pond. It was his red sailboat. Baby Pete was playing with it.

"Mine!" said Baby Pete.
"No, mine!" said Baby Mickey. Baby Mickey started to cry.
Baby Pete felt very sad. He gave the red sailboat back to Baby Mickey. "Sorry," he said. Then Baby Pete started to cry.
"Don't cry," said Baby Mickey. "Come with me."

Baby Mickey and Baby Pete took the red sailboat back to the other side of the pond.

"We can share," said Baby Mickey.

So Baby Mickey and Baby Pete shared the red sailboat. Baby Donald had a blue sailboat. Baby Minnie had a yellow sailboat. Baby Daisy had a green sailboat.

The five Babies put their sailboats into the water and gave each a little push.

"Hooray!" Baby Mickey and Baby Pete yelled together.

# Baby Brother Is Watching You

I have a baby brother.
I've never heard him quack.
Is he a real live duckling?
Or should I send him back?

When his bottle's empty,
All he does is cry.
Then he pulls my feathers.
I really don't know why.

He squirts me with his bottle,
And milk gets in my face.
I guess he's really not so bad.
I just may need some space.

## Teddy Bear

Baby Minnie was playing in her room. She was playing with all her new toys.

She opened her new music box. Music filled the room, and a little ballerina danced. She put a hand puppet on her hand. It was a green moose with red antlers.

Baby Minnie put on a puppet show for her new dolly in the green dress.

Suddenly Baby Minnie heard somebody crying. Who could it be? It wasn't her jack-in-the-box. It wasn't her horse. It wasn't her dolly.

Baby Minnie looked under her bed. She looked in her drawers. She looked under her table. But she couldn't see anyone crying.

Then she looked in her closet. The crying grew louder and louder.

It was coming from a box.

Baby Minnie opened the box and found her old teddy bear. Tears were coming from his eyes. He was really crying!

"Don't cry, Teddy," said Baby Minnie.

"I can't help it," said the teddy bear. "You never play with me anymore. You only play with your new toys. Boo-hoo-hoo!"

“I’m sorry,” said Baby Minnie. She held Teddy’s hand and took him out of the closet. She sat him in the middle of her room next to her new dolly in the green dress. She wiped the tears from his eyes.

Then Baby Minnie put on a puppet show for her old friend Teddy.

The teddy bear smiled. Baby Minnie smiled, too.

When Baby Minnie took her nap, she made sure Teddy Bear was on the pillow right beside her. Teddy would never be lonely again.

## At the Zoo

The giraffe
Doesn't laugh.

The gnu
is serious too.

The kangaroo
feels blue.

The crocodile
Doesn't smile.

But the hyena I'm after
is always filled with laughter!

# The Magic Carpet

Baby Gyro was making something special. He banged on a funny-looking ball with his hammer. He twisted nuts and bolts with his pliers.

Baby Mickey and Baby Goofy did not know what Baby Gyro was making with the big orange carpet. Besides, they were too busy playing peekaboo.

Finally Baby Gyro was all finished. "Sit," he told Baby Mickey and Baby Goofy.

Baby Mickey and Baby Goofy sat on the big orange carpet. Baby Gyro spun the funny-looking ball. "Fly! Fly!" said Baby Gyro. Suddenly the carpet flew into the sky.

"Gawrsh!" shouted Baby Goofy.

"Golly!" yelled Baby Mickey.

The magic carpet took the three Babies high in the sky.

Soon they flew over mountains covered with snow.

Baby Gyro spun the funny-looking ball. "Fly! Fly!" said Baby Gyro.

Soon the three Babies were flying over lots and lots of sand. The carpet landed in the desert. Baby Gyro, Baby Mickey, and Baby Goofy looked up and saw a big statue made of stone. The statue had the body of a lion and the head of a man. It was called the Sphinx.

"Hello," said Baby Goofy.

Baby Gyro spun the funny-looking ball. "Fly! Fly!" said Baby Gyro.

Baby Gyro spun the funny-looking ball. The magic carpet flew into the sky. Baby Gyro, Baby Mickey, and Baby Goofy flew over water. The magic carpet landed on top of a big whale.

The three Babies sailed on the back of the whale for a long time. Water sprayed out of the top of the whale, sending the magic carpet up in the air.

Baby Gyro spun the funny-looking ball. "Fly! Fly!" said Baby Gyro.

The magic carpet flew across the sky and landed on green grass. The three Babies were back in Baby Gyro's backyard.

"More!" said Baby Mickey.

"More!" said Baby Goofy.

Baby Gyro grabbed his hammer and his bucket of nuts and bolts. He showed Baby Mickey and Baby Goofy his plans to build something new.

"Rocket ship," said Baby Gyro.

"Fly! Fly!" shouted Baby Mickey and Baby Goofy. They could hardly wait for a ride on the Rocket Ship. Where do *you* think it will take them?

## Snow

Snowflakes can be orange,
Snowflakes can be pink.
Snowflakes can be purple
(My favorite, I think).

Snowflakes can be yellow.
There are many different types.
Snowflakes can have polka dots.
Or snowflakes can have stripes.

Where are all these snowflakes
With the colorful look?
You'll find them right in here —
In my coloring book.

# Lights Out!

The Babies were having a sleep-over at Baby Mickey's house. Everyone was in bed. Baby Mickey was sleeping with his teddy bear. Baby Goofy was sleeping with his head on the pillow. Even Baby Pluto was sleeping. But Baby Donald did not want to go to sleep.

Baby Donald looked around the dark room. There were shadows everywhere. The shadows moved. They were Baby Donald's shadows. But Baby Donald did not know that. He was scared. He wanted to go back to bed. But he could not find the bed in the dark.

Then Baby Donald bumped into something round and rubber. It rolled away. Baby Donald could not see what it was. He did not know it was just Baby Mickey's red rubber ball. He was scared. He wanted to go back to bed. But he could not find the bed in the dark.

Baby Donald crawled around on the floor. Then he bumped into a net. Baby Donald could not see what it was. He did not know it was just Baby Mickey's playpen. He was scared. He wanted to go back to bed. But he could not find the bed in the dark.

Suddenly Baby Donald felt something warm and wet on his face. He did not know what it was. He was scared. Then he turned around. He did now know it was just Baby Pluto licking his face. Baby Donald started to cry.

Baby Pluto jumped up and turned on the light. Baby Donald looked around the room. He saw Baby Mickey's ball, and the playpen, and Baby Pluto. Baby Donald stopped crying. He felt very silly. There wasn't anything scary in Baby Mickey's room.

Baby Donald turned off the light and got back in bed with Baby Mickey, Baby Goofy, and Baby Pluto. He wasn't scared of the dark anymore.

Little fingers,
Little toes,
Two bright eyes,
One small nose!

Put them together—
One, two, three—
And what you've got
Is little me!

## Good Night Bear

Go to sleep, my teddy bear!
I've sung enough lullabies!
All you do is stare at me.
You never close your eyes!

# The Three Wishes

Baby Minnie crawled through Mrs. Spencer's antique store. She found an old brass lamp. The brass lamp was dirty, so Baby Minnie rubbed it to make it clean.

Suddenly a cloud of smoke came out of the lamp. The cloud turned into a big genie with a beard and a green turban on his head.

"I am the genie of the lamp," said the genie. "I will grant you three wishes. What is your first wish?"

"Ice cream," said Baby Minnie.

*Poof!*

Baby Minnie looked around. She wasn't in Mrs. Spencer's antique store anymore. She was sitting on a small hill of vanilla ice cream. There was a river of chocolate syrup. There was a mountain of strawberries. Whipped cream floated in the river.

"Brrrr!" said Baby Minnie. She was very cold. She didn't want this much ice cream. It was too much. She started to cry.

"What is your second wish?" asked the genie.

"Toys," said Baby Minnie.

*Poof!*

Baby Minnie was warm again. She looked around. She was in the window of a toy store. She was standing on a music box with a beautiful ballerina.

The ballerina spun around and around to the music. Baby Minnie spun around, too.

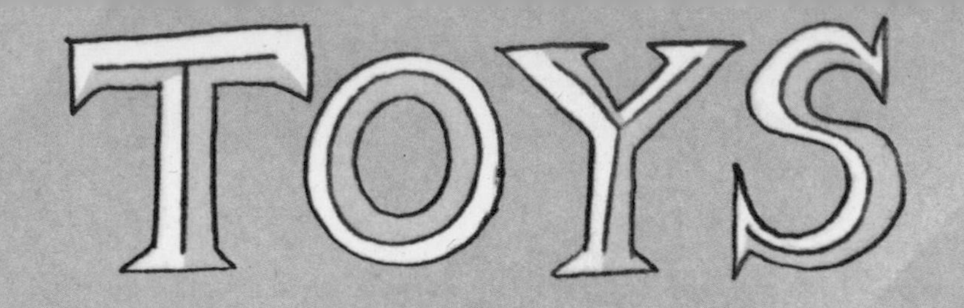


*Tap, tap, tap!* Someone was tapping on the window. It was a little girl looking in the window of the toy store. "I'll take that one," said the little girl, pointing at Baby Minnie. "I want to take her home."

"Oh, no!" said Baby Minnie. She was very sad. She didn't want to go home with the little girl. She started to cry.

"What is your third wish?" asked the genie.

"Back," said Baby Minnie.

*Poof!*

Baby Minnie looked around. She was back in Mrs. Spencer's antique store, holding the old brass lamp. She didn't see the genie anywhere.

"You can have that lamp if you wish," said Mrs. Spencer.

"No, thank you," said Baby Minnie. She was glad to be right back where she belonged.

# Sharing

"It's mine!" I said.
My face turned red
    When Daisy grabbed my choo-choo.

"I will not share.
I do not care
    If you scream till you turn blue."

I was mad.
Daisy was sad.
    She crawled under a table.

Then I gave in.
I just can't win!
    I guess I'm just not able.

She played awhile.
I saw her smile.
    She brought the choo-choo my way.

Sharing's not bad.
I guess I'm glad
    That both of us can play.

# The Playful Pup

The hands on the big clock said two o'clock. Baby Mickey was taking a nap. But Baby Pluto didn't know what time it was. He didn't know that Mickey was taking a nap. Baby Pluto only knew one thing. He wanted to play with somebody. So he decided to look for somebody to play with.

Baby Pluto ran outside as fast as he could. He ran and ran.

Baby Pluto didn't know where he was. He looked around and saw a park with flowers and trees. He ran inside.

But it wasn't a park at all. The sign said "Zoo." But Baby Pluto didn't know how to read the sign.

Inside the zoo there were many animals for Pluto to play with. But the giraffes were too tall, the elephants were too big, and the seals were too wet.

Then Baby Pluto found someone just right. He went into the petting zoo and found a baby goat. But the goat's favorite game was butting Baby Pluto with his head. That was too rough for Baby Pluto. So he said good-bye to the goat and ran back home.

When Baby Pluto got home, he was very tired.

Baby Mickey woke up from his nap. He was ready to play with Baby Pluto now.

But Baby Pluto needed to take a nap. From now on, he thought as he fell off to sleep, I'll play with someone my own size!

## Baby Talk

Sometimes I look
Like I'm happy.
And sometimes I look
Like I'm sad.
I can't really say
How I'm feeling today.
But I think my face
Tells you I'm glad.

## My Kitty

When my little kitty sees
Me down on my hands and knees,
I wonder if she's thinking that
I'm just another kitty cat!

# Afternoon in the Park

Baby Donald and Baby Mickey went to the park one sunny day. Baby Mickey brought his purple pail and shovel.

Baby Donald and Baby Mickey could not choose what to do first. Should they play in the sandbox? Should they go down the slide? Should they go on a seesaw? Should they watch the frog, the fish, and the turtles?

Baby Mickey started crawling toward the seesaws.

"No!" yelled Baby Donald. He tried to pull Baby Mickey back.

Baby Donald wanted to play in the sandbox first. He grabbed the purple pail and shovel.

"No!" yelled Baby Mickey. He held on to the purple pail and shovel very tightly.

Baby Mickey was angry. Baby Donald was angry.

So they each decided to play alone.

Baby Mickey went on the swings by himself. But there was no one to push him.

Baby Donald played in the sand by himself. But there was no one to help him build a sand castle.

Baby Mickey decided to play with his red ball. But there was no one to play catch with him.

Baby Donald crawled over to the seesaw. But there was no one to sit on the other end and make it go up and down.

Baby Mickey wasn't having very much fun.

Baby Donald wasn't having very much fun either.

Baby Mickey went looking for Baby Donald.

Baby Donald went looking for Baby Mickey.

When they found each other, they started laughing.

"This is silly!" said Baby Donald.

"Let's just have fun, okay?" said Baby Mickey.

Together they climbed on the seesaw. Now they could both ride up and down.

After a while they tossed the red ball back and forth. Then they pushed each other on the swings. Then they built a castle together in the sand.

"Hooray!" shouted Baby Mickey and Baby Donald. "It's much more fun to play together!"

## My Silly Friend

I have a silly friend
High above my head.
He always comes out late at night
When I'm tucked in my bed.

So I sleep all night through,
Until night goes away.
Then the moon, my silly friend,
Goes home to sleep all day.

# Baby Goofy and the Beanstalk

Once upon a time Baby Goofy dug a hole in the dirt with his shovel and hoe. He planted some magic green beans in the ground. Then he waited for the beans to grow.

All of a sudden, a big, fat beanstalk shot up from the ground. It grew taller and taller and taller, all the way up to the clouds.

Baby Goofy was sitting on a leaf. It carried him up to the clouds with the beanstalk.

At the top of the beanstalk was a very strange land. Everything was very, very big. There was a big stone house. Inside, Baby Goofy found giant tables, giant chairs, and giant cups and saucers.

Suddenly Baby Goofy heard giant footsteps. He was scared. So he crawled inside a giant slipper.

"Fee-Fie-Fo-Fum! I smell a baby sucking his thumb!" said the giant.

Baby Goofy crawled out of the slipper. The giant was very, very big.

"Gawrsh," said Baby Goofy.

"Fee-Fie-Fiddle-De-Diddle! Answer me this giant riddle!" said the giant. "What kind of bow can't be tied or untied?"

Baby Goofy thought and thought. But he did not know.

Baby Goofy was afraid the giant might eat him all up.

He was very scared. He wanted to go home. He looked out the window and saw a rainbow.

"Rainbow!" said Baby Goofy.

"Yes, little baby," said the giant. "A rainbow cannot be tied or untied."

The giant laughed and laughed. "You are a funny little baby," said the giant. "Do you want to go home now?"

"Yes!" said Baby Goofy.

The giant picked up Baby Goofy in his hand, reached through the clouds, and lowered him to the ground. Then the giant pulled the beanstalk up from the ground and into the clouds.

And now every time Baby Goofy sees a rainbow, he thinks of his friend the giant who lives in the clouds.

# Good Night

Now it's time to say good night
To you, our little friend.
We're sure you know the reason why—
Because this is . . . THE END!